A Little Salmon for Witness

A STORY FROM TRINIDAD

by VASHANTI RAHAMAN

illustrated by SANDRA SPEIDEL

LODESTAR BOOKS
Dutton   New York

Library of Congress Cataloging-in-Publication Data

Rahaman, Vashanti.
A little salmon for witness:
a story from Trinidad / by Vashanti Rahaman;
illustrated by Sandra Speidel.—1st ed.
p.   cm.
Summary: On Good Friday, a school holiday
in Trinidad, Rajiv spends the day searching
for a special birthday present for his grandmother.
ISBN 0-525-67521-3
[1. Grandmothers—Fiction.   2. Trinidad and
Tobago—Fiction.   3. Islands—Fiction.
4. Gifts—Fiction.   5. Birthdays—Fiction.]
I. Speidel, Sandra, ill.   II. Title.
PZ7.R1272Li   1997
[E]—dc20
95-726

Published in the United States by Lodestar Books,
an affiliate of Dutton Children's Books,
a division of Penguin Books USA Inc.,
375 Hudson Street, New York, New York 10014

Published simultaneously in Canada
by McClelland & Stewart, Toronto

Editor: Virginia Buckley
Designer: Marilyn Granald

Printed in Hong Kong   First Edition
10 9 8 7 6 5 4 3 2 1

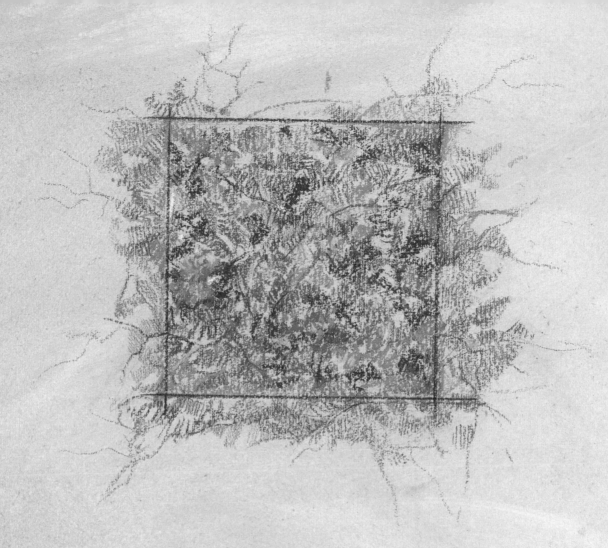

Aaji's birthday came on Good Friday this year. It was here already, but Rajiv did not have his present for her yet. Luckily, Good Friday was a school holiday in Trinidad, the Caribbean island where Rajiv lived.

Yawning, he ducked under the half curtain of faded pink net and leaned over the windowsill. Aaji had let him sleep late, and the sun was up, warming away the morning chill.

"It don't look like you'll get rain today, Aaji," he called to his grandmother.

Aaji was in the backyard picking spinach for supper.

"Well," she said, "I'll just have to write today's date on an empty bottle." She gathered her pile of spinach into a bundle and took it into the kitchen.

"Why your *aaji* does collect rainwater on Good Friday?" asked Robert from the next yard.

"I don't know," said Rajiv. "She say it is special water. You know how it is—every special day always have a set of foolishness some people does do."

"Them special days would be nothing without what you call a set of foolishness," said Robert. "Now, for me, Good Friday is a day to go fishing. You want to come?"

Rajiv laughed. "For you," he said, "every holiday is a day to go fishing. No thanks! Fishing and me don't agree. I can never catch anything."

"Rajiv!" Aaji called. "Come for your breakfast."

While Rajiv drank a cup of cocoa and ate a few crackers, Aaji began picking the old leaves and hard stems out of the spinach.

"So," she said, "what you doing today since you have no school?"

"If it's okay with you," said Rajiv, "I was thinking to practice cricket in the savannah with the school team." Near the savannah was a good place to look for the present he planned for Aaji.

"Well," said Aaji, "go play if you want, and take a hops bread and cheese for lunch. But make sure you come back by three o'clock so you could study your books a little before darkness fall."

Rajiv cut open a round, hard roll and slipped in a slice of cheese. Then he put his sandwich in a paper sack.

"Happy birthday, Aaji," he said. "I'll be back around two-thirty."

"What birthday?" said Aaji. "All I have to prepare for supper is *dhaal* and rice and *bhaajee*, without even a little tin of salmon for witness."

Every day they had boiled rice and *dhaal*, a split pea gravy, and *bhaajee*, the spinach. But Rajiv didn't mind. Even *bhaajee* tasted good when Aaji cooked it.

On special days, they might have something extra—a witness. It could be a couple of pieces of curried chicken backs and necks, or a slice of fried fish, or a spoonful of a second vegetable. But things had been especially bad lately. Often there was only hot pepper for witness.

"In my youth," said Aaji, as she washed the spinach, "on Good Friday everyone in the village used to eat smoked salmon, well cooked up with onions and tomatoes. You couldn't have Good Friday without that. Never mind. Things change. Now smoked salmon is king and emperor. I have no hope of tasting it again. Only rich people can afford that. Even tinned salmon is The Honorable Mr. Salmon." She laughed a sad and bitter laugh. "Don't mind me, boy," she said. "Go and play your cricket."

Until this morning, Rajiv would not have thought of giving Aaji salmon for her birthday. For him, eating salmon on Good Friday was just another bit of foolishness attached to another special day. He could see now, though, that it meant much more than that to Aaji.

Rajiv went out the kitchen door. He had been looking forward to playing cricket, but a tin of salmon—a little tin—would make Aaji's day.

Of course, Rajiv didn't have any money. He had been planning to pick an armful of wildflowers and grasses and pods for Aaji. There were plenty growing in the abandoned sugarcane fields near the savannah where he played cricket. It would cost only a little of his time, and Aaji always needed things she could dry for the fancy wreaths and other decorations that she made to sell.

Salmon cost money, though. Maybe one of the neighbors would give him a tin if he did some small jobs.

"So what happen, boy, you get too big to tell people 'morning' now?" Miss Jean was in the road cleaning the gutter outside her house. Rajiv had nearly bumped into her.

"Sorry, Miss Jean," said Rajiv. "I was just wondering . . . You think you could give me a tin of salmon if I clean the gutter? How all that rubbish get there?"

"It's the nasty habits some people in this street have," said Miss Jean. "They does treat the road like a dumpster or something. But no, boy. I would give you the salmon if I had it. I know you want it for your *aaji*. But I don't have any, even for myself, this year."

Rajiv went right past Robert's mother's house. She was always happy to help Aaji, but she didn't have salmon this year. Instead, she was cooking soup with a big red-fish head and a lot of potato and green banana and pepper. He had heard her tell Aaji about it.

At the next house, Sookdeo's mother was making *pelau* to take to the beach. The rice and pigeon peas and well-seasoned chicken steamed together in a big iron pot. It filled the house with a delicious smell.

She didn't have any salmon. "The children and their father doesn't eat the salmon when I makes it," she said. "So I stop getting it at all."

"You want to come with we by the sea?" asked Sookdeo's father. "Go ask your *aaji*. It have plenty of room in the van, and plenty *pelau*."

A day by the sea was tempting, and so was the *pelau*.

"No thanks," said Rajiv slowly. "Aaji wants salmon. I have to find a way to get some for her."

"Why you don't ask Miss Khan?" asked Sookdeo mischievously.

"You know," said Rajiv, "I think I will ask her."

"Well, you must really want that salmon," said Sookdeo.

Children stayed away from old Miss Khan, and it wasn't just because of her three big German shepherd dogs. Even the beggars who came down the street every morning never stopped at her gate. She was too stingy and disagreeable to give anybody anything. She sat all day in her huge, ancient house and spied on people through the slats of her wooden shutters.

I am not asking her to give me the salmon for free, thought Rajiv as he walked down to Miss Khan's house. I am asking to work for it.

The German shepherds barked and snarled as soon as they saw Rajiv. He jumped back and then walked up and down outside the gate, wondering what to do. The dogs would bite him if he tried to rattle the gate. Perhaps he should try shouting.

"Good morning!" Rajiv called, as loud as he could. "Good morning, Miss Khan!" He could barely hear himself above the barking of the dogs, but he felt sure that the old lady was peeping at him from one of her windows. She knew who he was—she knew everyone on the street—and if he kept calling, she was bound to get curious.

After a long while, Miss Khan opened a window and shouted, "What you doing here, boy? You should be in school."

She closed the window before Rajiv could remind her that it was a school holiday.

"Miss Khan!" Rajiv called again.

She stuck her head out of another window. This time she had a telephone receiver in her hand. "I am calling the police for you. Instead of going to school, you come round here harassing me."

Miss Khan was always complaining about people harassing her. Sometimes, though, the police came when she called. Rajiv did not want to stay around for them to take him home and tell Aaji that he had been bothering Miss Khan. Some birthday present that would be!

Rajiv was ready to give up and go play cricket. After the game, he could pick something for Aaji's dried arrangements. That would make her happy enough. It wasn't as though he had promised her the salmon. She wasn't even expecting it.

Still, it didn't feel right to give up yet. Besides, if he was busy working for someone when the police came, they would leave him alone.

By this time, Rajiv had reached Ma Ben's house. As he went by, he saw her weeding the yard. It reminded him of something, but he couldn't think what, so he stopped and watched her for a while. Her yard was as neat as a calendar picture. She was so particular about things, Rajiv thought. Surely she would get salmon for Good Friday, even if it meant going without something else.

"Morning, Ma Ben," said Rajiv respectfully. "I am looking for a job to do. I could clean your yard for a tin of salmon."

"You want salmon?" said Ma Ben. "I only have smoked salmon. You know what that costs?"

Smoked salmon would be really special. Aaji would be overjoyed. "I will do plenty, plenty work," said Rajiv eagerly.

"Child," said Ma Ben. "I don't have plenty work for you. Besides, the piece of salmon I have is too small to share. Sorry, child."

Rajiv decided he was in no mood to play cricket after all. Maybe, if he couldn't get the salmon, he should go home and do some chores for Aaji. That might be a better present than a bundle of grasses she would rather pick herself. She was very careful about choosing the right material for her handicraft.

Ma Ben had gone back to her weeding. What did that remind him of? It was annoying not to remember.

Then it came to him. Of course! Teacher Omar and his Ti Marie problem!

Teacher Omar lived with his wife and baby in one of the new town houses near the savannah. His house had only a little piece of yard with no fence, and even that small yard was giving Teacher Omar trouble. Just the other day, he had complained that his lawn was full of Ti Marie, a weed that their science book at school called The Sensitive Plant. Rajiv had boasted that Ti Marie would be no problem to him at all.

Ti Marie was fun for little children to play with when it grew wild in the bush. Sometimes even Rajiv enjoyed going from plant to plant, touching the small, feathery leaves and watching them close up instantly. When Ti Marie, with its tiny, purple, puffball flowers invaded a lawn, however, it spread like a carpet—a carpet full of thorns. Mowing the lawn only made it spread more.

Teacher Omar would be at the teachers' cricket match, but perhaps his wife was at home. Maybe, if Rajiv dug out the Ti Marie for her, she would give him a tin of salmon. Teachers were rich, thought Rajiv. They didn't buy things one at a time. They bought by the dozen. People who could afford it might eat salmon often, not just on Good Friday.

Rajiv smoothed his hair and tucked in his shirt. Then he reached through the locked wrought iron gate to knock at the front door of the town house.

Teacher Omar's wife peeped through the iron grille on the window and asked, "What do you want, boy?"

"Good morning, Schoolmistress," he began.

Teacher Omar's wife smiled, and Rajiv felt more confident. Calling her Schoolmistress was a piece of old-time foolishness—so, in fact, was saying "Teacher Omar" instead of "Mr. Omar." Most grown-ups seemed to like that kind of thing, though. It made them smile.

"Good morning, Schoolmistress," said Rajiv again.

"Talk, child," said Teacher Omar's wife. "I won't bite you."

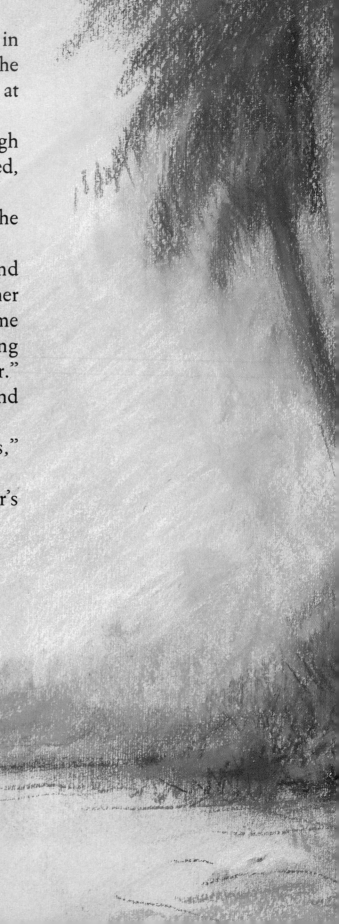

"Please, Schoolmistress," said Rajiv. "Teacher Omar said the other day in science class that he was having trouble with Ti Marie. There was a picture of Ti Marie in the book, you see. I thought that, maybe, you would let me dig it out of your lawn for you."

"How much are you asking for the job?" asked Teacher Omar's wife.

"No money, Schoolmistress."

"No money!" She paused and examined him for a while. "You want food, then?"

"Yes, Schoolmistress," said Rajiv, relieved that she had understood. "It is Aaji's birthday today, Good Friday, and we don't even have the spare change to buy a small tin of salmon."

"What! Do you think I have a shop here or something? I only have two tins of salmon, and your teacher could eat a tin by himself."

"It's okay," said Rajiv, sadly. "It's just that Aaji is so unhappy about the salmon, and I thought . . ."

"That I would have at least a dozen tins?" asked Teacher Omar's wife gently. "Well, maybe I would if this place had more cupboards. Come, I will pay you with money. Then you can buy the salmon."

"No thanks, Schoolmistress," said Rajiv. "You see, if I get money, I will have to take it to Aaji. She wouldn't want me to spend it on salmon."

Teacher Omar's wife sighed. "Okay," she said at last. "If you dig out the Ti Marie, I will give you some of my salmon. We really only need it for a little witness to the rice and *dhaal,* and I can cook more *bhaajee.*"

Rajiv was surprised that teachers ate like poor people. Maybe they didn't make so much money after all.

The lawn was very tiny, a little square patch as wide as the front of the narrow town house. But the thorny branches of Ti Marie crept everywhere. Rajiv had to lift those branches one by one until he found where each root went into the ground. Then he took Teacher Omar's big knifelike cutlass and dug the roots out. It was hard work. The cutlass was too big, as long as his leg from knee to ankle. The Ti Marie scratched his hands and feet.

At lunchtime, Teacher Omar's wife asked if he wanted something to eat. When she saw his cheese and bread, she handed him a little box of cold milk through the locked gate. Rajiv had never had one of those boxes before, though he had seen other boys bring them to school. If he hadn't been so sore and tired and hungry, he would have sipped it slowly to make the treat last longer.

At three o'clock, Rajiv finally finished the job He could hear the church clock ringing the hour.

Teacher Omar's wife peeped through her iron bars and inspected Rajiv's work. She nodded in approval when he pointed to the huge heap of Ti Marie that he had dumped in the empty lot next to the town houses. "Well, boy," she said, "give me your lunch bag."

She filled the paper sack and handed it back to him through the iron gate. "There!" she said. "Bless you! You are a good grandson."

Rajiv took the bag, and his heart sank. He could tell that, whatever was in the bag, there was no tin of salmon. It would not do, though, to argue with a teacher's wife. If she complained about it to Teacher Omar, who knows what would happen to him at school? Then, too, she might even threaten to call the police like Miss Khan did. So he forced a smile and, muttering his thanks, went sadly on his way.

When he was well out of sight of the town houses, he opened the bag and looked in. What he saw was almost too good to be true. He let out a whoop of joy and raced home.

Aaji was pacing on the rickety front veranda. She started fussing as soon as she saw Rajiv. "What happen, boy? I was so worried. I thought I told you to come home before three o'clock. Where you was? What happen to your hands? Don't tell me . . ."

"Nothing bad happened," said Rajiv, "but look at what I have here."

Still fretting, Aaji inspected his prize and gasped.

Without saying another word, she went into the kitchen.

Slowly, smiling with wonder, she emptied the little bag. In it was a five-dollar bill, a small onion, a tomato, and, carefully wrapped in plastic, a little piece of smoked salmon—for witness.